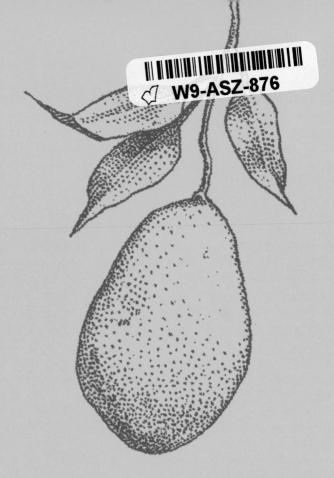

Stellaluna

J A N E L L   C A N N O N

Houghton Mifflin Harcourt

BOSTON   NEW YORK

Bonus crafts and activities!
www.hmhbooks.com/freedownloads
Access code: BAT

With thanks to Dr. Nancy Simmons, Curator-in-Charge,
Department of Mammalogy, American Museum of Natural History,
for her expertise and assistance with the Bat Notes.

www.hmhco.com

The illustrations in this book were done in Liquitex acrylics and Prismacolor pencils on bristol board.
The display type was hand-lettered by Judythe Sieck.
The text type was set in Guardi #55.

Library of Congress Cataloging-in-Publication Data
Names: Cannon, Janell, 1957- author.
Title: Stellaluna / Janell Cannon.
Description: Boston ; New York : Houghton Mifflin Harcourt, [2018] |
Originally published in 1993 by Harcourt Brace Jovanovich. | Summary:
After she falls headfirst into a bird's nest, a baby bat is raised like a
bird until she is reunited with her mother.
Identifiers: LCCN 2016013602 | ISBN 9780544874350 (hardcover)
Subjects: LCSH: Bats—Juvenile fiction. | Birds—Juvenile fiction. | CYAC:
Bats—Fiction. | Birds—Fiction.
Classification: LCC PZ10.3.C1685 St 2017 | DDC [E]—dc23
LC record available at https://lccn.loc.gov/2016013602

Manufactured in China
SCP 16 15 14 13 12 11 10 9
4500775128

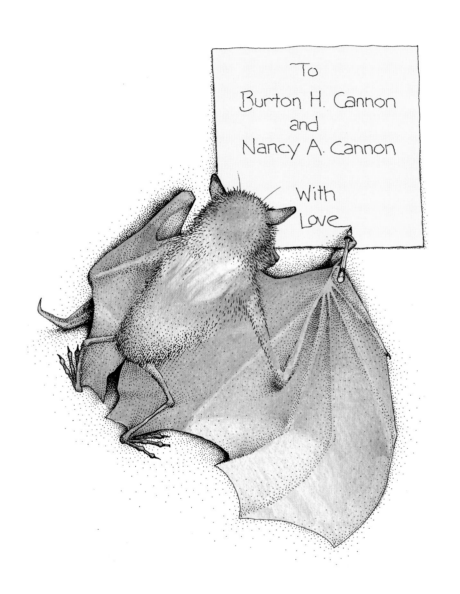

To
Burton H. Cannon
and
Nancy A. Cannon

With
Love

In a warm and sultry forest far, far away, there once lived a mother fruit bat and her new baby.

Oh, how Mother Bat loved her soft tiny baby. "I'll name you Stellaluna," she crooned.

Each night, Mother Bat would carry Stellaluna clutched to her breast as she flew out to search for food.

One night, as Mother Bat followed the heavy scent of ripe fruit, an owl spied her. On silent wings the powerful bird swooped down upon the bats.

Dodging and shrieking, Mother Bat tried to escape, but the owl struck again and again, knocking Stellaluna into the air. Her baby wings were as limp and useless as wet paper.

Down, down she went, faster and faster, into the forest below.

The dark leafy tangle of branches caught Stellaluna as she fell. One twig was small enough for Stellaluna's tiny feet. Wrapping her wings about her, she clutched the thin branch, trembling with cold and fear.

"Mother," Stellaluna squeaked. "Where are you?"

By daybreak, the baby bat could hold on no longer. Down, down again she dropped.

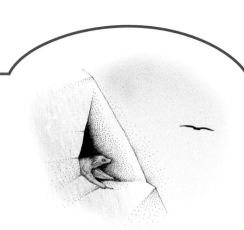

Flump! Stellaluna landed headfirst in a soft downy nest, startling the three baby birds who lived there.

Stellaluna quickly clambered from the nest and hung out of sight below it. She listened to the babble of the three birds.

"What was *that?*" cried Flap.

"I don't know, but it's hanging by its feet," chirped Flitter.

"Shhh! Here comes Mama," hissed Pip.

Many, many times that day, Mama Bird flew away, always returning with food for her babies.

Stellaluna was terribly hungry—but *not* for the crawly things Mama Bird brought.

Finally, though, the little bat could bear it no longer. She climbed into the nest, closed her eyes, and opened her mouth.

Plop! In dropped a big green grasshopper!

Stellaluna learned to be like the birds. She stayed awake all day and slept at night. She ate bugs, even though they tasted awful. Her bat ways were quickly disappearing. Except for one thing: Stellaluna still liked to sleep hanging by her feet.

Once, when Mama was away, the curious baby birds decided to try it too. When Mama Bird came home, she saw eight tiny feet gripping the edge of the nest.

"Eeeek!" she cried. "Get back up here this instant! You're going to fall and break your necks!"

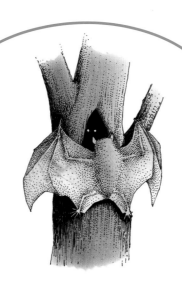

The birds clambered back into the nest, but Mama Bird stopped Stellaluna. "You are teaching my children to do bad things. I will not let you back into this nest unless you promise to obey all the rules of this house."

Stellaluna promised. She ate bugs without making faces. She slept in the nest at night. And she didn't hang by her feet. Stellaluna behaved as a good bird should.

All the babies grew up quickly. Soon the nest became crowded.

Mama Bird told them it was time to learn to fly. One by one, Pip, Flitter, Flap, and Stellaluna jumped from the nest.

Their wings worked!

I'm just like them, thought Stellaluna. *I can fly too.*

Pip, Flitter, and Flap landed gracefully on a branch.
Stellaluna tried to do the same.

How embarrassing!

I will fly all day, Stellaluna told herself. *Then no one will see how clumsy I am.*

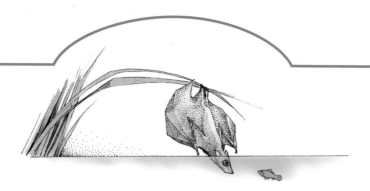

The next day, Pip, Flitter, Flap, and Stellaluna went flying far from home. They flew for hours, exercising their new wings.

"The sun is setting," warned Flitter.

"We had better go home, or we will get lost in the dark," said Flap.

But Stellaluna had flown far ahead and was nowhere to be seen. The three anxious birds went home without her.

All alone, Stellaluna flew and flew until her wings
ached and she dropped into a tree. "I promised not to
hang by my feet," Stellaluna sighed. So she hung by her
thumbs and soon fell asleep.

She didn't hear the soft sound of wings coming near.

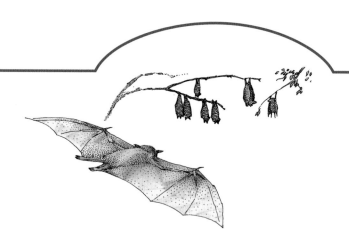

"Hey!" a loud voice said. "Why are you hanging upside down?"

Stellaluna's eyes opened wide. She saw a most peculiar face. "I'm not upside down. *You* are!" Stellaluna said.

"Ah, but you're a *bat*. Bats hang by their feet. You are hanging by your thumbs, so that makes you *upside down!*" the creature said. "I'm a bat. I am hanging by my feet. That makes me *right-side up!*"

Stellaluna was confused. "Mama Bird told me I was upside down. She said I was wrong . . ."

"Wrong for a bird, maybe, but not for a bat."

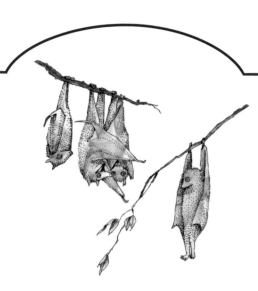

More bats gathered around to see the strange young bat who behaved like a bird. Stellaluna told them her story.

"You ate *b-bugs?*" stuttered one.

"You slept at *night?*" gasped another.

"How very strange," they all murmured.

"Wait! Wait! Let me look at this child." A bat pushed through the crowd. "An *owl* attacked you?" she asked. Sniffing Stellaluna's fur, she whispered, "You are *Stellaluna*. You are my baby."

"You escaped the owl?" cried Stellaluna. "You survived?"

"Yes," said Mother Bat as she wrapped her wings around Stellaluna. "Come with me, and I'll show you where to find the most delicious fruit. You'll never have to eat another bug as long as you live."

"But it's nighttime," Stellaluna squeaked. "We can't fly in the dark, or we will crash into trees."

"We're bats," said Mother Bat. "We can see in darkness. Come with us."

Stellaluna was afraid, but she let go of the tree and dropped into the deep blue sky.

Stellaluna *could* see. She felt as though rays of light shone from her eyes. She was able to see everything in her path.

Soon the bats found a mango tree, and Stellaluna ate as much of the fruit as she could hold.

"I'll never eat another bug as long as I live," cheered Stellaluna as she stuffed herself full. "I must tell Pip, Flitter, and Flap!"

The next day Stellaluna went to visit the birds.

"Come with me and meet my bat family," said Stellaluna.

"Okay, let's go," agreed Pip.

"They hang by their feet and they fly at night and they eat the best food in the world," Stellaluna explained to the birds on the way.

As the birds flew among the bats, Flap said, "I feel upside down here."

So the birds hung by their feet.

"Wait until dark," Stellaluna said excitedly. "We will fly at night."

When night came, Stellaluna flew away. Pip, Flitter, and Flap leaped from the tree to follow her.

"I can't see a thing!" yelled Pip.

"Neither can I," howled Flitter.

"Aaeee!" shrieked Flap.

"They're going to crash," gasped Stellaluna. "I must rescue them!"

Stellaluna swooped about, grabbing her friends in the air. She lifted them to a tree, and the birds grasped a branch. Stellaluna hung from the limb above them.

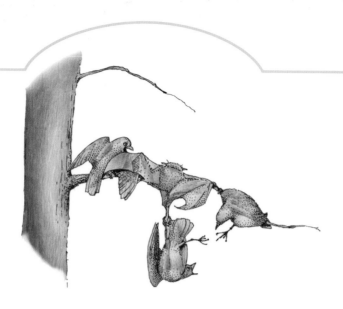

"We're safe," said Stellaluna. Then she sighed. "I wish you could see in the dark too."

"We wish you could land on your feet," Flitter replied. Pip and Flap nodded.

They perched in silence for a long time.

"How can we be so different and feel so much alike?" mused Flitter.

"And how can we feel so different and be so much alike?" wondered Pip.

"I think this is quite a mystery," Flap chirped.

"I agree," said Stellaluna. "But we're friends. And that's a fact."

BAT NOTES

Of the nearly 5,500 species of mammals on Earth, almost one-quarter (more than 1,370 species) are bats, the only mammals capable of powered flight.

The scientific name for bats is *Chiroptera,* "hand-wing," because the skeleton that supports the wing is composed of the animal's hand and elongated finger bones.

Most bats use echolocation in order to navigate in flight, avoid obstacles, and detect and track prey. Echolocation is a form of biological sonar—using sound to sense the world around us. There are over 1,100 species of echolocating bats, and they live in every climate around the world except the polar zones. Many eat insects, while others feed on fish, amphibians, reptiles, and even other mammals. Still other echolocating bats feed on fruit or the nectar and pollen of flowers. Some of the most famous are vampire bats, of which there are only three species. Vampire bats can be found from Mexico to Argentina. They prey primarily on domestic cattle and native mammals and birds, from which they obtain blood meals through tiny bites. Contrary to myth, no bats are blind.

However, not all bats echolocate. Most Old World fruit bats, like Stellaluna, instead use their keen vision and sense of smell to orient themselves and find their food. There are about 200 species of Old World fruit bats. The smallest have a wingspan of 11 inches. The largest have a wingspan of nearly 6 feet. Old World fruit bats generally have long muzzles, large eyes, pointy ears, and furry bodies, which is why they are often called flying foxes. They live in tropical and subtropical climates that provide year-round supplies of their favorite fruits, flowers, and nectar. Some fruit bats, as they forage for nectar, pollinate many types of night-blooming trees and plants. Others eat whole fruits, seeds and all, and distribute the seeds over the forest floor in their droppings. In these ways, bats are very important to the regeneration of tropical forests.

More Books by
JANELL CANNON

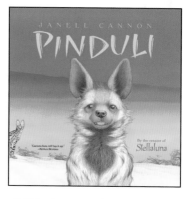

★ "Glorious."

—*Publishers Weekly,* starred review

★ "Inspiring."

—*Booklist,* starred review

"Hilarious and endearing."

—*School Library Journal*

Coloring Sheet

Crossword Puzzle

Solve the clues below to reveal character names and anim...

Friendship Bracelets

Cut out the bracelets below. Wrap around a wrist and tape to secure.

It's fun to hang with friends!

I go out on a limb for my friends!

On the look for new fri...

We're friends. And that's a fact.

Stellaluna Matching Game

Print these two pages on card stock using a color printer. Carefully cut the cards on the dotted lines.

INSTRUCTIONS

Shuffle the cards. Place the cards face-down on a table or the floor, arranging them in five rows, each with four cards. Players take turns turning over two cards. If the pictures on the cards don't match, the player replaces the cards face-down. Then it's the next player's turn. If the pictures match, the player keeps the cards and selects two more cards. The player with the most pairs at the end of the game wins!

Stellaluna Matching Game
2-3 players

Don't miss the downloadable craft and activity kit!

www.hmhbooks.com/freedownloads

Access code: BAT

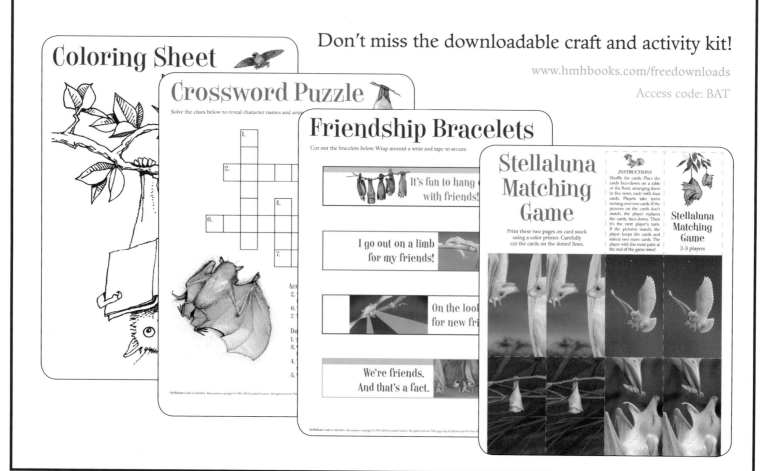

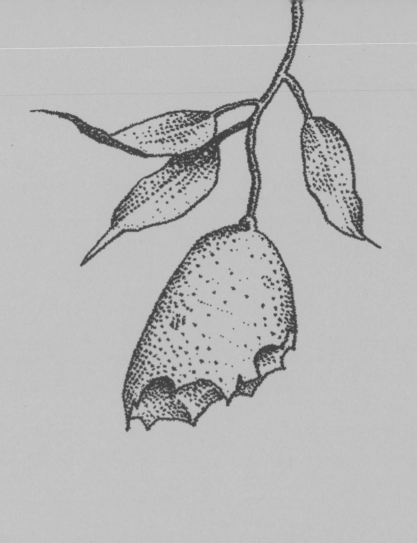